Grandma McGarvey Goes to Sea

First published by Ashton Scholastic, 1994

Ashton Scholastic Ltd
Private Bag 92801, Auckland, New Zealand

Ashton Scholastic Pty Ltd
PO Box 579, Gosford, NSW 2250, Australia

Scholastic Inc
555 Broadway, New York, NY 10012-3999, USA

Scholastic Canada Ltd
123 Newkirk Road, Richmond Hill, Ontario L4C 3G5, Canada

Scholastic Publications Ltd
7-9 Pratt Street, London, NW1 0AE, England

Text © Jenny Hessell, 1994
Illustrations © Trevor Pye, 1994
ISBN 1-86943-258-4

9 8 7 6 5 4 3 2 1   4 5 6 7 8 9 / 9

Edited by Penny Scown
Typeset in 16/18pt Bembo by Typeset Graphics Ltd
Printed in Hong Kong

Grandma McGarvey Goes to Sea

Story by Jenny Hessell
Illustrated by Trevor Pye

Ashton Scholastic
Auckland Sydney New York Toronto London

When Grandma McGarvey needed a rest,
(she had a bad cold and a pain in her chest)
she didn't sip lemon or take to her bed
or stretch herself out on the couch.
Instead...

she loaded the car with nautical gear—
a piratical parrot, some bottles of beer,
a compass, a cutlass, a couple of pails

and a hammock that Grandpa had bought at the sales.
(The strings, she noticed, were not very tight
so her bottom was sure to poke through in the night!)

Then she gave a sly smile and did a wee jig.
"This could be the start of something big,"
she said, as she plastered her nose with zinc.

And what do you think?

It was.

When Grandma McGarvey rode out on the tide,
she stood at the helm with the dog at her side
and she gazed at the compass and called to the crew,
"Ahoy there, me hearties! There's work we must do.
All hands to the wheel! Let's give this a crack."

But the dog looked as if he would rather turn back,
as he slunk from the deck and hid under the stair
and the parrot turned surly and started to swear.

So Grandma McGarvey trimmed all the sails,
checked out the rigging and banged in some nails.

Then, high on the mast, she narrowed her eyes
as she noticed the waves were beginning to rise
and threatening clouds were starting to form...
"I hope we're not heading straight into a storm,"
she said, as her heart began to sink.

And what do you think?

They were.

When Grandma McGarvey sailed into the squall,
torrents of rain were beginning to fall,

and the waves reared up and came thundering down,
while the parrot was shrieking, "We're going to drown!"
and the dog was whimpering under the stair
and the sails were straining and threatening to tear.

Then the boat started pitching from starboard to port,
and the parrot (who wasn't the sea-faring sort)
clung to her shoulder with squawks of alarm,
turned terribly green and was sick down her arm,
and the dog (whose eyes were bulging with shock)
did something disgusting all over her sock.

"At least," said Grandma, stifling a curse,
"Things couldn't possibly get any worse."
(And she pinched her nose to block out the stink.)

But what do you think?

They did.

When Grandma McGarvey opened her eyes,
the waves had returned to a comfortable size.

So she tidied the deck and straightened the sails
and bailed out the boat with the battered old pails.

And when it was done, she muttered, "At last!
I think we can say that the danger has passed."

"Think again!" shrieked the parrot and pointed its wing
and Grandma beheld the most terrible thing...

Her knees began knocking, her eyes opened wide —
a man-eating shark had loomed alongside.

Its skin was all slimy, its eyes were blood red,
and razor-sharp teeth flashed white in its head
as it opened its mouth with a gluttonous grin,
swooped on the deck and sunk its jaws in.

Then Grandma shouted, "We're not finished yet!
I'll teach you a lesson you'll never forget!"

She grabbed for the rail, reared up on her toes, and whacked a pail down hard on its nose.

And before the shark could get itself free,
Grandma McGarvey went down on one knee
and wound the hammock around it tight.
(And its bottom stuck through, as she thought that it might.)

Then Grandma McGarvey said with a smile,
"Now that should shut you up for a while,"
(as she fastened the lock with a flourishing clink).

And what do you think?

It did.

When Grandma McGarvey headed for home,
she soared on the waves, and she flashed through the foam.
And when she came within sight of the land
she could see on the jetty a gathering band.
They were clapping and shouting and raising a cheer:
the townsfolk, the councillors — even the mayor!

So Grandma McGarvey blew them a kiss.
"They'll probably give me a medal for this,"
she said, as she waved and slipped them a wink.

And what do you think?

THEY DID!